THE SHADE
OF DEATH

HAWKITE
ARROW OF
THE AIR

With special thanks to Lucy Courtenay

For George H and Dominic McN

www.beastquest.co.uk

ORCHARD BOOKS
338 Euston Road, London NW1 3BH
Orchard Books Australia
Level 17/207 Kent St, Sydney, NSW 2000

A Paperback Original
First published in Great Britain in 2009

Beast Quest is a registered trademark of Working Partners Limited
Series created by Beast Quest Limited, London

Text © Working Partners Limited 2009
Cover and inside illustrations by Brian@KJA-artists.com
© Orchard Books 2009

A CIP catalogue record for this book is available from
the British Library.

ISBN 978 1 40830 438 9

8

Printed in Great Britain by CPI Group (UK) Ltd, Croydon, CR0 4YY

The paper and board used in this paperback are natural recyclable
products made from wood grown in sustainable forests. The
manufacturing processes conform to the environmental regulations of
the country of origin.

Orchard Books is a division of Hachette Children's Books,
an Hachette UK company

www.hachette.co.uk

HAWKITE
ARROW OF
THE AIR

BY ADAM BLADE

ORCHARD

*W*elcome to a new world...

Did you think you'd seen all the evil that existed? You're almost as foolish as Tom! He may have conquered Wizard Malvel, but fresh challenges await him. He must travel far and leave behind everything he knows and loves. Why? Because he has six Beasts to defeat in a kingdom he can't even call home.

Will his heart be in it? Or will Tom turn his back on this latest Quest? Little does he know, but he has close ties to the people here. And a new enemy determined to ruin him. Can you guess who that enemy is...?

Read on to see how your hero fares.

Velmal

PROLOGUE

The field lay devastated. The crops
were flattened to the ground, and
good for nothing. Harvin and his
father walked through the broken
wheat stalks, gazing at the remains
of the harvest.

"I can't believe it," Harvin's father
groaned. "Another ruined crop."

It was too much. They couldn't go
on like this. Harvin knew his father

had nothing left to sell. Their barn
was empty, their livestock long gone.
Everywhere in Gwildor, people were
desperate for food. And now this...

Harvin's stomach growled hungrily.
"What will we eat tonight?" he asked.

His father shook his head. "I don't
know," he said. "These storms...
They come from nowhere and ruin
everything."

He fell silent and Harvin knew that
his father was thinking of how they
had so nearly lost their farmhouse
in the night. The wind had torn at
the roof shingles and battered the
windows until the panes of glass
had shattered.

The air suddenly grew cold. A
shadow fell across the ruined field,
passing over Harvin and his father.
They looked up and fell to their

knees in terror. Something was flying overhead. Even though it was high in the sky, its vast wings cast a shadow that ran from one end of the field to the other. It looked like a hawk. But it couldn't be – it was too big, and its bald head was like that of a vulture.

The Beast screamed in fury. Harvin flinched as it swooped downwards. Its gigantic shadow grew closer. Everything turned black as it plummeted towards them.

Now they could see its cruel talons, razor-sharp, angled towards them. A vile stench, like dead flesh, made Harvin gag and cover his nose. The Beast continued to swoop down, cutting through the air like a black arrow. Harvin could see its evil eyes, glinting red. Something was glowing on the underside of one wing – green feathers, strange and out of place on the immense fiery-coloured bird.

"We're going to die!" whispered Harvin. He grasped his father's hand and trembled with terror.

The Beast beat its mighty wings and the wind struck them like a sledgehammer. Trees on the edges of the field crashed to the ground, splintering in the force of the gale. The last crops were torn up by their roots and flung into the air. Harvin managed to grab onto a fence post. He clung to it as the wind tried to rip the clothes off his back. He could feel his father's grip on his other hand loosening as the wind tugged at him. It was no good. His father couldn't hold on.

The Beast beat its wings again. The powerful wind picked up Harvin's father as if he were made of straw and threw him against a tree. There was a sickening snap. The man fell to the ground in a crumpled, broken heap.

Sobbing with terror, the boy clung onto the post. The raging Beast was swooping lower. The wind from its wings screamed in Harvin's ears. He buried his head in the crook of his arm, and wished this was all a dream. But he knew it was real. There would be no waking up.

CHAPTER ONE

THE CHALLENGE BEGINS

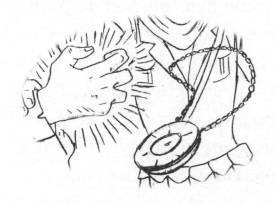

The emerald-green sea lapped at the Gwildorian shore. Tom and his three companions – his best friend, Elenna, Storm the stallion and Silver the wolf – gazed out at the waves, marvelling at the richness of their colour.

Tom could hardly believe they were still alive after their terrible battle with Gwildor's first Beast, Krabb.

His right hand throbbed, reminding him of the confrontation beneath the waves. Tom had broken evil Wizard Velmal's curse over the giant crab, and Krabb had returned to protecting Gwildor again. But Tom knew this was only the beginning: five more Beasts dwelt in Gwildor, and all of them were under Velmal's spell. If Gwildor was to survive, Tom and Elenna had to free them all.

But it wouldn't be easy. Freya, Gwildor's Mistress of the Beasts, had turned against her land and was working with Velmal – which meant that this was their most dangerous Beast Quest yet.

Tom flexed his aching palm, testing it. Pain rippled through him. A strange green bruise had appeared on Tom's hand where Krabb had grasped him with his poisoned pincer.

"I wish Aduro and Taladon had told us what kind of Beast was next," said Elenna, testing the sharp tips of the arrow-heads with her thumb. Her silver-coated wolf growled gently at her side.

Tom smiled at the mention of his father: Taladon, Avantia's Master of the Beasts. Free at last from Malvel's evil magic, Taladon was now working with the good wizard, Aduro, to keep Avantia safe.

"They told us as much as they could," Tom reminded Elenna, reaching out to stroke the rough fur on Silver's head.

Elenna looked around. "There's something strange about this place," she said. "It seems *too* beautiful, somehow."

"Gwildor and Avantia are twin realms," said Tom. "I think we'll get used to it in time."

"We had better," said Elenna, putting the arrows back in her quiver. "If Gwildor falls, Avantia will be next."

Tom nodded. "Let's move on," he said. He touched the silver Amulet of Avantia that hung around his neck. On his last Beast Quest, to Avantia's Forbidden Land, he had recovered all six pieces of the amulet to restore full life to his father, Taladon, who had been trapped as a ghost. Looking down at it, Tom admired the way the blue disc at the centre of the amulet glinted and shimmered. He turned it over, tracing the magical map of Gwildor that was etched on the back – they weren't completely lost while they had this.

A sharp pain stabbed through his arm and the amulet fell from his hand. If only he hadn't let Krabb catch him with his poisonous pincer!

"Are you all right, Tom?" Elenna asked in concern.

Tom forced a smile. "Don't worry about me," he said.

Beside Tom, Storm tossed his head and whinnied. Reaching out with his good hand, Tom stroked his stallion's jet-black mane. "It's all right, boy," he soothed. "We've been through worse, haven't we? It's time to find the next Beast of Gwildor."

Tom held up the Amulet again, keeping it as steady as he could. He watched as two red paths appeared on the etched map, glowing and pulsing. Tom knew that one path would lead to the Beast. The other would lead to a prize that would help them on their Quest: one of the magical items owned by the Mistress of the Beasts, before wicked Velmal had placed her under an evil enchantment.

"What is the amulet showing you?" Elenna asked,

Tom pointed out the two red paths shimmering on the silver talisman. Unlike the Quest to find Krabb, both lines led in the same direction. "Look," he said, pointing at the tiny picture etched where both paths ended. "Sheaves of corn – farmland."

"But there's no picture of the Beast that we have to face," Elenna said worriedly.

"We have to trust the amulet," Tom replied, letting it dangle again. "It showed us Krabb last time, and I'm sure it will show us the new Beast when it's ready."

Tom climbed into Storm's saddle. His hand flamed with pain, but he tried not to wince. Leaning down, he gingerly pulled Elenna into the saddle behind him. The animals

seemed to sense the urgency of the
Quest – Storm pawed the ground and
Silver paced about, letting out a low,
rippling growl. Tom wheeled Storm
about and they headed inland.

Although he tried to focus on the challenge that lay ahead, Tom couldn't help remembering their visit from Velmal after they had arrived. Freya, Gwildor's Mistress of the Beasts, had been with the evil, flame-haired wizard. Tom shuddered as he thought of her savage eyes and pitch-black hair. It was because of Freya that Gwildor was in this peril. Tom knew he should hate her – but he also knew that Freya was under Velmal's control, just like the Beasts of Gwildor. There was something about her... Tom had felt drawn to her, and he didn't know why.

He shook his head, feeling impatient with himself. Now was not the time to dwell on the past. They had a Beast to find – and set free.

CHAPTER TWO

SEARCHING FOR THE PRIZE

Gwildor rolled away from them in a sheet of green, blue and gold. Elenna gasped in delight, twisting round in the saddle to take in their surroundings.

"It's so beautiful!" she murmured. "Look at the colours!"

Tom had to admit, Gwildor was even more beautiful than Avantia.

The colours were richer, the air was purer. Even the clouds that scudded overhead in the deep blue sky seemed whiter than white.

He turned to look over his shoulder at Elenna. "There's something about this place," he said, searching for the words. "This Quest feels like the most important one we've ever faced."

"All our Quests have been important," Elenna pointed out.

"Yes, but..." Tom stopped. He didn't know how to explain it to Elenna, but freeing the Beasts of Gwildor somehow felt *personal*.

They reached the head of a valley, and the view took Tom's breath away. The rolling hills were a deep, emerald green, and a foaming turquoise river thundered between rocks. It was truly the most beautiful place he'd ever seen.

They made their way down the valley, checking the amulet to be sure they were going the right way. Elenna gasped at the pretty birds that wheeled in the sky. The flowers by the wayside seemed to pulse with colour. Silver sniffed them and sneezed as the bright yellow pollen tickled his nose.

They reached the far side of the valley as the sun began to set. The rich fingers of golden light seemed to set the whole land on fire. Tom pulled Storm up on the mossy riverbank.

"Let's stop here for the night," he suggested to Elenna.

Silver had already padded over to a springy patch of pea-green moss and was settling down.

"Silver thinks that's a good idea,"

Elenna chuckled. "I'll gather wood, if you make a fire."

Tom tethered Storm to the coppery trunk of a hazel tree. He then prepared the fire with the wood that Elenna found. Soon the flames cast light and shadow over the camp. Even fire had an extra brightness here in Gwildor.

They ate their bread and cheese, and the full white moon above added its light to their campfire. As Elenna stoked the flames, Tom took out the amulet and studied the map.

Now they were further inland, the paths were twisting off in slightly different directions. One led towards a village with rounded roofs, and the other led among the etched sheaves of corn Tom had seen earlier.

Elenna looked at Tom. "Which path should we take?" she asked.

Tom knew that they needed to find Freya's prize first. If his experience with Krabb was anything to go by, the prize would give him a magical skill that he could use to defeat the next Beast. He gazed more closely at the map. At the end of the path that led to the farmland he noticed a tiny image of what looked like a bird. Beneath the bird was some small writing. Tilting the amulet to the fire, he saw that it read *Hawkite*.

"This must be the Beast," said Tom, pointing out the bird picture to Elenna. He followed the other path into the village with his finger. "And here's a ring – look," he said, his finger coming to rest on a miniature etched circle. "It must be the prize!"

Silver padded out of the darkness, where he had been hunting for food. Storm stood quietly, still chomping the lush Gwildor grass at his feet.

"We'll find it tomorrow," said Elenna sleepily, lying down and throwing her arm over the warm body of her wolf. "Goodnight."

Soon, Tom could tell from her light breathing that she was asleep.

As he lay his own head on the ground, he wished he could rest so easily. But his mind was too full of thoughts. What would this Beast be like? Could they prevail? And why did Gwildor feel so strange, and yet so familiar?

The moon was waning before Tom drifted off. His dreams were vivid, filled with images of Freya, Velmal, and the shadowy outline of a Beast in the form of a bird...

Hawkite.

They had barely emerged from the valley the next morning when they arrived at a fork in the road. One path snaked away into the hills. The other led straight ahead.

"A signpost would be helpful,"

Elenna joked, as Tom brought Storm to a halt.

Tom stared at the well-worn paths and reached around his neck for the amulet. His hand hurt more today, and the green bruise was slightly darker. But before he could take out the amulet and study the map, Storm was pulling at his reins. Tom looked up.

Silver had trotted up to the fork and was sniffing the ground. Without hesitating, the wolf loped down the left path. He stopped and gazed calmly at the others over his shoulder.

"Silver wants us to follow him," said Tom, as Storm pulled at his reins again. They were lucky to have such instinctive animal friends.

Tom tapped Storm's flanks with his heels. With a snort, Storm broke into a trot down the left-hand path, which was lined with hedges.

"Look at that!" Elenna pointed at a glossy red robin hopping through the hedgerow. "It's so bright, it looks like it's had an extra layer of paint or something!"

They rounded a corner. The hedge fell away, revealing a collection of small thatched houses gathered in a circle around a pond. The golden straw roofs were bright and neat, and the small village pond was a deep sapphire blue. Somewhere, among those houses, was the ring that Tom had to find.

Tom nodded and smiled in greeting as brightly-clothed villagers emerged from their houses to stare at him and his friends.

"Please, don't be afraid," Elenna

said, as the villagers flinched away from her great silver wolf. "He's friendly."

No one smiled back. Tom noticed that despite the brightness of the villagers' clothes and the neat appearance of their houses, their faces were sallow-skinned and

sunken. Their clothes hung from
their thin, scarecrow-like bodies.
Dark shadows lay beneath their eyes.

Tom and Elenna shared a startled
glance.

"These people are starving!" he told
her under his breath.

CHAPTER THREE

THE PAINTED TRUTH

The villagers shuffled towards them.
Storm backed away, shaking his
mane. Tom grabbed hold of the
stallion's reins.

More villagers spilled out of their
houses. Tom narrowed his eyes as he
looked at them. He knew desperate
people were capable of desperate
acts...

Soon Tom and Elenna were surrounded. Silver growled. Elenna slipped out of the saddle behind Tom and pulled her wolf close. Several of the villagers were staring at Storm and Silver with hungry eyes. They looked as if they would kill and eat both animals, given half a chance.

"Look what the wind's blown in," a man's voice called from somewhere at the back of the crowd. The villagers shuffled closer. Skinny hands reached out. Storm flinched and Tom vaulted out of his saddle.

"We've come to help you," he said into the silence.

"No one can help us!" said the man who had spoken first. His voice was bitter. The crowd murmured in agreement, and stepped closer to Tom and Elenna.

"Make way!" shouted a quavering voice somewhere at the back of the throng. "Out of my way, now. Welcome! Welcome!"

Muttering, the villagers drew back. Tom saw a shrivelled old woman in a bright purple dress pushing through to the front. The fabric hung in empty folds over her bony frame. Her sunken eyes burned intensely at Tom, as if she recognised him from somewhere. She shuffled towards Tom and Elenna. From the way the villagers bowed their heads respectfully, Tom guessed she was the chief of the village.

"Come!" the old woman said in a cracking voice. "You are welcome and under my protection."

She seized Tom and Elenna with a surprisingly firm grip. The villagers broke apart and returned to their brightly coloured homes. Tom glanced back over his shoulder as the old woman dragged them towards her house. He caught several resentful stares. They had clearly made enemies in this stricken place. Holding tightly to Storm's reins, Tom let the old lady pull them onwards. He knew they should be grateful for her help.

"Come this way." The old woman kept glancing back at Tom and smiling. "Not far now..."

Tom and Elenna shared a glance.

"I hope we're doing the right thing," Elenna whispered.

Tom hoped so, too. But what choice did they have? They couldn't stay with those desperate villagers.

The old woman's house was at the

end of the village. A small stable stood
behind the little thatched dwelling.
The old woman urged Tom to stable
Storm – "He will be safe, my dear, safe
as can be..." – and then pushed him
through the door of her cottage.
Elenna and Silver followed, ducking
beneath the overhanging thatch.

Inside, the cottage was dark and
warm, and a pitifully thin gruel
bubbled over the hearth.

Tom frowned as he looked at their host. How much should he tell her about their Quest?

"Speak," said the old woman calmly. "You search for something, don't you?"

Elenna gasped. "How...?"

Tom was startled, too. "Yes," he said at last, realising that he had no choice but to trust her. "A ring. We think it is here in the village. Do you know where we might find it?"

It seemed an impossible question. If anyone in this village knew the whereabouts of a precious ring, they would have sold it to buy food. But Tom's Quest meant he needed to find out.

"Of course," the old woman nodded. "In the painting."

Tom glanced at Elenna. Elenna

shook her head, looking as confused as Tom felt. *What painting?*

"Come," said the old woman, moving towards the ladder in the corner of the room.

Tom and Elenna followed. Silver lay on the floor, waiting for them to return.

At the top of the ladder was a dusty attic room. Cobwebs draped between the beams like veils and at the far end hung an ugly yellow sheet. Elenna glanced at Tom and raised her eyebrows. "That's no painting," she murmured in a low voice.

The old woman took the corner of the sheet and pulled it aside with a flourish. A large picture was revealed, propped up against the wall. Painted on what looked like silk, the picture showed a boy and a girl. Tom stared in shock. Thoughts whirled through his head. The boy had brown hair, a sword and a shield. The girl had a quiver of arrows on her back. But – it was impossible! They looked just like him and Elenna.

Tom looked more closely. The boy held his sword in his left hand – and Tom was right-handed. Apart from that, the resemblance was astonishing. Tom reached cautiously towards the painting. He ran his fingers down the boy's arm until he reached his hand.

Tom started as a second wave of shock hit him. The boy was holding a ring in his right hand, and the ring was dripping with water. The boy's eyes seemed to seek out Tom's, challenging him. *The ring...*

The old woman was nodding and smiling at him encouragingly.

Gathering his wits, Tom looked at
Elenna.

"Do you see that?" he said,
pointing at the ring.

"It's dripping water..." Elenna
murmured, frowning. Then the two
of them cried out at the same time:
"The pond!" The painting was telling
them the magic ring's hiding place.

"Come on," Tom said, running
back towards the ladder.

45

"You've found what you were looking for, then?" the woman called after them as Tom climbed onto the top rungs of the ladder.

"Yes, thank you!" he said, before scrambling down to a waiting Silver. There was no time to lose. He was certain that the magic ring was hidden in the sapphire-blue water of the village pond.

Before Tom could run out of the house, the old woman climbed stiffly down the ladder and put a bony hand on his shoulder.

"It's you, isn't it?" she said. A feverish look came into her eyes. "The boy from the painting. You've come to us at last."

Tom gently took her hand and shook his head.

"I'm sorry," he said. "It looks like

me but I don't see how it can be.
We must go now." Elenna was right
behind him, and Silver yapped
impatiently at her heels. Tom raced
for the door, and out into the bright
daylight. He had to find the ring.

Their Quest depended on it!

CHAPTER FOUR

THE SECRET IN THE POND

Tom and Elenna dodged past a couple of startled villagers and ran on towards the centre of the village and the blue pond.

"The painting!" Elenna was panting as she caught up with Tom. Silver loped easily beside her. "It was *us*, Tom. What did the old woman mean, 'you have come at last'? The boy from the coast recognised you, too. He said you were the one from the prophecy."

"I can't think about this now, Elenna," said Tom, shaking his head. "The ring – we have to find it!"

They reached the pond. It glinted in the sun. It was hard to tell how deep the water was; the centre of the pond was so dark it was almost black. There were no ducks and no fish. Tom suspected they had long since been eaten by the villagers. He was still shaken by the old woman's words, and the uncanny painting. Something strange was happening in Gwildor. But he had to concentrate. There was a prize to find.

Tom took off his sword and shield, preparing to dive into the water. He thrust them at Elenna. He felt in his pocket for the magic pearl and took it out. This prize had helped him defeat Krabb, by allowing him to breathe underwater, and he knew that it would help again now. He ran towards the pond and jumped in. The shock of the cold water was intense and he rose to the surface, spluttering and splashing. He was aware of the villagers gathering curiously around the water's edge.

"What's he doing?" he heard one say. "The boy's crazy!"

More people were gathering. Some laughed. Tom saw Elenna watching anxiously from the edge. Tom ducked his head below the water. The pearl felt warm in his hand as the magic began to work. Breathing freely, Tom kicked downwards and started feeling around in the muddy silt at the bottom of the pond. A tiny fish

darted out from the reeds, a flash of
bright orange in the murk.

Something glinted. Tom pounced.
Pulling and tugging at the reeds, he
heaved the plants up by the roots. A
ring twinkled at him, spinning gently
in the disturbed water. Tom grabbed
it. Breaking the surface, he placed the
pearl in his pocket and held up his
new prize in triumph.

The ring felt heavy and cold in his hand. It was a brilliant gold, with the letter 'F' etched repeatedly all the way around it.

F... Freya.

Marvelling at how tiny the ring was, Tom carefully slid it onto his little finger. It fitted snugly.

"I have the ring!" Tom called happily, swimming over to the edge of the pond. "The ring – I've found it!"

Elenna leaned over and grabbed Tom's arm. She helped him out of the water, tugging as he slithered over the muddy edge of the pond and back onto dry land. The villagers crowded around them. Suddenly, Tom felt the point of a dagger being thrust into the small of his back.

"Hand it over," growled the knife-bearer, digging harder. Tom felt the blade pierce the back of his tunic.

"Tom!" Elenna cried, struggling in the grip of two other men. Silver barked madly but there were too many people in the way. He was powerless to protect his mistress.

Tom was dragged away from the water's edge. The crowd jostled around him, jeering and shouting as he was marched across to the village hall with his hands behind his back. A big man stood at the doorway, winding a length of rope around his fists.

"Give us the ring," snarled the knife-bearer. He brought his blade up to Tom's throat. "It's ours. It was found in our pond."

"No," Tom said stubbornly. He flinched as the blade drew a drop of blood.

"Can't you see how hungry we are?" demanded the man with the rope. "We can sell it. We can buy food. If you don't hand it over, I'll make you..." He stepped up to Tom, twisting the rope tighter. His meaning was unmistakable.

"Food!" cried the crowd. "Give us the ring! The ring!"

In the background, Elenna was fighting hard, but her captors were holding her too firmly.

Across the village square, Storm
whinnied. Tom turned quickly, and
saw three men leading the stallion
towards the pond. Anger flashed
through him. They had stolen Storm
from the old woman's stable! Storm
struggled, bucking and baring his
teeth, but he was unable to pull free.

Tom knew he couldn't give up the
ring. He *needed* it to defeat Hawkite.
Then he remembered the magic pearl.

He didn't need to breathe underwater any more. Could he offer that to the villagers instead?

Part of him resisted. The pearl had belonged to the Mistress of the Beasts. *Why should I hand it over?* he thought angrily to himself.

But it was the only choice he had.

Putting his hand in his pocket, he drew out the pearl. He held it high, so the crowd could see it. The sunlight made it shine and its smooth surface rippled with light. The villagers stepped forward greedily.

"You can have this," Tom said, "if you let me keep the ring."

"Take it!" the villagers shouted, gazing at the shining orb. "Take it!"

The knife-bearer removed his blade from Tom's throat and held out his hand for the pearl. Tom passed it over.

The hungry villagers pushed him aside as they ran towards the market square. There wasn't much food left and it was very expensive, but at last the villagers could afford it.

Storm trotted across the empty street towards Tom, his reins trailing behind him. His captors had let him go without a second thought.

"Thanks, Tom," said Elenna gratefully, running towards him with Silver at her side. Her captors had let her go as they headed for the market with the rest of the villagers. She frowned as she stroked Silver's head. "I know you had to give them the pearl, but it feels wrong. We need all the magic we can get right now."

"I didn't know what else to do,"

Tom admitted. "But they let us go, and that's what counts."

He scooped up Storm's reins and pulled himself into the saddle. Pain shot through his injured hand. Elenna swung up behind him on Storm's back and Silver barked joyfully as Tom twitched the reins. The stallion broke into a gallop, with the wolf running easily alongside.

"I had no choice, Elenna," Tom called back over his shoulder as they galloped away from the village and back down the lane, with its high green hedges. "We just have to hope that I'll get the pearl back one day. But for now – let's find this Beast!"

CHAPTER FIVE

FIRST GLIMPSE

Tom reined in Storm as they reached
the fork in the road once again.
The golden ring glinted on his little
finger. In the intense Gwildor light,
it was dazzling.

"What do you think the ring's
magic is, Tom?" Elenna asked,
echoing Tom's own thoughts.

"I don't know," Tom said honestly.

"I don't feel any different since putting it on."

He slid out of the saddle and lifted the silver amulet from inside his tunic. The fingers on his injured hand were too numb to clasp it. He held it carefully in his palm and gazed at the etched map. One path had disappeared. The other – the one leading to farmland – glowed more brightly than ever. Tom stared intently at the tiny etched image of Hawkite. How could he tackle this Beast?

Silver gave a confused bark.

"Tom?" said Elenna. She sounded scared. "Tom, where have you gone?" Tom lifted his head. "I'm right here," he said in surprise.

Elenna gasped. "You... But you weren't there a moment ago!" she said, looking confused. "How—"

"The ring," Tom guessed. He smiled. "Now we know its magic! When I'm moving, you can see me. When I stand still – I disappear."

He held himself as still as he could. Elenna's mouth dropped open. She looked from left to right. Silver neighed anxiously. "You've disappeared again," she said.

Tom moved his arm very slowly. "Can you see me now?" he asked.

"Still can't see," Elenna said with a shake of her head. Then Silver padded over to Tom and sniffed at his ankles.

Tom moved normally, reaching down to ruffle the wolf's head. Elenna's eyes sharpened and focused on him again.

"The animals weren't fooled for

long," Tom said. "I don't think I actually disappear. I just – blend into the background. Like a chameleon."

He stood still again for a moment. Looking down at himself, he could see that his clothes had turned greyish. He looked over his shoulder and saw the exact same shade of grey on a stretch of rock behind him. He started to laugh. He could see how useful this might be in defeating the Beast.

"Let's go," he said, seizing a handful of Storm's mane and pulling himself up into the saddle with Elenna. He wheeled the stallion around so that Storm was facing the right-hand fork in the road. "Hawkite is waiting!"

This road twisted away from the village, heading deep into the farmland. The earth kicked up by Storm's hooves was heavy and rich – perfect for growing crops. So why was there so little food in this part of Gwildor? It didn't make sense.

The tall green hedgerow ended abruptly on one side of the road. It looked as if someone had torn it down and trampled on it.

"Did the Beast do this?" Elenna asked, gazing at the broken hedgerow.

Tom stared through the wreckage of the hedge to the field beyond. "Look," he said grimly, dismounting from Storm.

The field ahead of him was completely destroyed. The crops had been brutally torn up by the roots and scattered in all directions. Now they lay dying on the ground. The scene of devastation reminded

Tom of a hurricane.

"Do you remember what that villager said about the wind blowing us in?" Tom said. His eyes settled on the prone body of a farmer lying crumpled at the foot of a tree on the far side of the field. His head hung from his neck at a crooked angle. Even at this distance, it was clear that he was dead. "The Beast – Hawkite – must create this wind. People are dying. We have to stop this, now."

Tom watched as Elenna's eyes swept across the field. The wind had ripped up everything that they might be able to use as cover.

"Where is this Beast hiding?" she asked. "How are we going to lure him out? And where will *we* be able to hide? We can't fight him in the open. Not if he controls this wind.

We'll be blown away like feathers."

Storm whickered gently in Tom's ear as Tom stared at the horizon. He could just make out a strange shape, hunched close to the ground. It looked like an enormous rock. Not for the first time, he wished he still had the magical eyesight granted to him by Avantia's golden armour. But he had lost that when he battled with Stealth.

Tom squinted in the bright light. The rock moved. He saw the outline of a beak. It was silhouetted against the sky, razor-sharp and deadly. He felt a rush of terror and determination all at once. *Hawkite!*

"There," he said, pointing.

Elenna gasped as the Beast shifted its position. Fiery feathers gleamed evilly in the sunlight.

Tom winced as the Beast raised its ugly, bald head and gave a harsh, grating cry that seemed to shake the ground they were standing on.

He swallowed. "It's the biggest bird I've ever seen," he said.

"We can defeat it," said Elenna. Only the wobble in her voice told Tom that she was as nervous as him.

Tom touched his magic shield and belt. He may have lost the powers of the golden armour, but there were other skills he could draw on. The amber jewel in his belt from Tusk gave him extra-special fighting skills.

And I'm going to need all the help I can get, he thought to himself.

Hawkite stretched her mighty wings and flapped them lazily. They stretched across the horizon like a great slab of sheer rock blocking out the light. A strong wind whipped up across the field, almost knocking Tom and Elenna to the ground. Elenna cried out in alarm. Tom staggered and righted himself, gripping Elenna's arm. He shuddered as he realised the power of the creature before them.

Hawkite had almost thrown them off their feet with the wind created from the flapping of her giant wings – and she hadn't even seen them yet. What would she do when she knew she was being attacked? Tom felt a rush of fear. This creature was more powerful than even Epos or Spiros – the two great bird Beasts he had already defeated. He would have to

70

be extra-cunning to defeat her. A plan began to form in his mind...

He pulled Elenna back behind the hedgerow. "I think I know what to do," he said. "But you need to be brave."

Elenna smiled. "I'm always brave," she pointed out.

Tom wondered if his idea might be too much, even for someone with Elenna's courage. "I want to use you as a lure," he said. He turned to look at his friend. "Hawkite will come closer if she sees a girl standing alone in the field. She won't suspect a trap. With my new invisibility powers, we can use the element of surprise to attack her. But everything depends on you, Elenna. Will you do it?"

CHAPTER SIX

THE TRAP

Uncertainty flickered across Elenna's face. Tom held his breath.

"Glad to be of service!" she said, and broke into a smile.

Tom breathed out with relief. Elenna was the bravest person he'd ever met. He was lucky to have her as a friend. He peered back out at the field. Hawkite was still squatting on the horizon like a thundercloud.

"Come on then," Tom said, taking Elenna by the hand. "There's no time to lose."

He and Elenna walked away from the shelter of the hedge. They stepped into the devastated field, still holding hands. Silver and Storm followed, keeping close behind them. Storm flared his nostrils. An unpleasant stench was drifting towards them from the direction of the Beast. Animals knew that smell, and feared it.

It was the scent of death.

Tom glanced left and right. Out here, there was no cover. If his plan went wrong... He steeled himself not to think that way. Elenna needed him to stay focused.

As they neared the middle of the field, Hawkite raised her head. Tom froze, but the bird wasn't looking in their direction. A gobbet of meat was hanging from her beak. Tom shuddered as he thought of the poor creature that had become the Beast's meal. Tossing the last scrap of bloody gore into the air and snapping it up, Hawkite stretched her immense wings again and hopped away, over the brow of the field and out of sight.

Tom felt a jolt. Those wings were even bigger than he had thought. When Hawkite saw him and Elenna she would sweep them away like ants with one downward stroke of those feathers.

Tom knew at once that he'd never faced a Beast like this and he was risking his friend's life into the bargain.

He spun round and gripped Elenna by the shoulders. "You don't have to do this," he said. "It's so dangerous, Elenna. I can't let you risk it."

Elenna's face set into a stubborn expression. "I'm not backing out of it now," she said. "And nor are you."

They had reached the middle of the field. Elenna took her quiver of arrows from her back and put them at her feet. Now she was defenceless.

Tom nodded, biting his lip. He knew Elenna was right. They must do everything in their power not to hurt the Beast. He glanced back at the brow of the field. No sign of the giant bird. Trying not to think of how he might feel if Hawkite suddenly rose into view with her wings fully outstretched, he grabbed a handful of Storm's mane and pulled himself back up into the saddle.

"Good luck!" he called to Elenna, as

he dug his heels into the horse's flanks. Storm sprang away.

Silver ran gracefully by the stallion's side, barking and glancing back at Elenna once or twice. Elenna stood still among the broken cornstalks and watched them go. She looked very small. Was the Beast watching her?

As he galloped for cover, Tom could almost feel that sharp beak at his neck and smell the Beast's meaty breath. But somehow they safely reached the far side of the field. Hawkite had not yet come.

Dismounting, Tom left Storm grazing and waited behind a broken piece of fencing. From this distance, Elenna looked smaller and more defenceless than he'd ever seen her. The sky remained still. A gentle breeze blew through the branches of the last remaining tree on the edge of the field. In the silence, Tom heard his heart beating.

Would the Beast fall into their trap?

"Come on," Tom muttered to himself, staring at the last place he'd seen the Beast. He gripped the fencing with his good hand. His magic ring glinted in the light. "Show yourself, Hawkite!"

Leaves swirled at Tom's feet, making him jump. The temperature dropped as something shut out the sun's rays and sent heavy black shadows in its place. A great blast of fetid air lifted Tom off his feet. It slammed him into the remains of the fence he had been holding. Splinters ripped into his exposed skin.

Dazed, he slid to the ground. He shook his head to clear it and twisted round to see Elenna. She was staring up at the sky in terror.

Tom looked up as well. At first he could see nothing. Darkness stretched across the sky. With a thrill of horror, Tom realised he was looking at the underside of Hawkite's wings. They stretched from one side of the field to the other.

The Beast was coming.

CHAPTER SEVEN

PLAYTIME

Hawkite circled overhead, screeching wildly. Her wings were so huge that it was as if night had fallen over the Gwildorian field. The stench was overwhelming. Tom caught a glimpse of the glowing eyes in the creature's monstrous bald head as Hawkite peered down at her prey. Elenna remained motionless, like a mouse held in the gaze of a hunting bird.

The Beast flapped her great wings, hovering in the air just like a hawk.

Hawkite shrieked and swooped. Elenna threw herself to the ground. The wind was intense. The Beast caught Elenna in her talons, then dropped her. Elenna screamed. But it seemed the Beast was only playing with her – for now...

All thoughts of his plan vanished
from Tom's head. He could only
think of getting his friend away from
the Beast.

"Elenna!" he yelled, struggling
forward. The wind from the Beast's
wings made it difficult, and he
lurched to one side. "Run!"

Silver barked wildly, and ran towards his mistress. The wind tore through his rough coat, pushing him back. The wolf stumbled, wrong-footed. Storm bucked and reared, shaking his glossy black head.

Elenna looked as if she was in a trance. She was on her knees, gazing at the Beast overhead, watching Hawkite's every twist and turn. It was as if the Beast had hypnotised her.

Realising that Elenna was too scared to move, Tom jumped over the fence and started running towards her. The wind buffeted him mercilessly. More than once he stumbled and fell. The smell was nauseating. With Silver at his side – and Storm too, lashing out with his front legs – Tom found the strength to get up again. "Run, Elenna!" he shouted. But she couldn't hear him through the scream of the wind.

Hawkite moved overhead like an immense shadow of death. Gazing up, Tom glimpsed several strange green feathers on the underside of one of her wings. They glowed with unmistakeable evil.

The Beast had adjusted her wings, bringing them closer to her sides; she had finished playing and she plummeted from the sky, her talons angled and ready to slice into Elenna's flesh and lift her up and away. With one last desperate lunge, Tom reached Elenna and pushed her out of Hawkite's reach. He grabbed his sword. Pain lashed through his arm. He stared in dismay at his sword hand as he struggled to grip the handle of his weapon and pull it

from its scabbard. The green bruise
from Krabb's poisonous pincer had
spread, working its way towards
his wrist.

Tom's actions had snapped Elenna
out of her trance. "Tom!" she
screamed, reaching for her quiver
of arrows.

But there was no way even Elenna
could put an arrow to her bow and
shoot it at the Beast in time. Was
this it – their last Quest? Right here
and now?

Tom forced his fingers to grip the
hilt of his sword, despite the
throbbing ache of the green bruise.
He yanked his sword roughly out of
its scabbard, struggling to hold it
upright. *Come on!* he told himself, as
he glanced up to see the Beast diving
towards Elenna, eyes blazing. Why

couldn't he move faster – now, when it really counted?

Then, at the last moment, Hawkite pulled out of her dive. She soared upwards, screeching at the sky.

"She's still toying with us," Tom shouted. Fury raced through him as he watched her wheel above their heads. "Elenna, get out of the field. Take Storm and Silver with you. This is my fight."

Elenna nodded and fitted an arrow to her bow. She took aim as the Beast circled lazily, higher and higher. Hawkite was preparing to dive again. "I'll cover you!" she shouted, backing away as she held her bow steady. "Silver! Storm! With me!"

Tom flexed his hand, trying to ease his muscles as Storm and Silver raced after Elenna. His tendons flamed with pain. But at last he was gripping his sword, pointing it towards the Beast.

Hawkite dropped like a stone. One minute she was a speck of black in the sky, high above. The next, she

Tom touched his magic shield and belt. He may have lost the powers of the golden armour, but there were other skills he could draw on. The amber jewel in his belt from Tusk gave him extra-special fighting skills.

And I'm going to need all the help I can get, he thought to himself.

batted ferociously across the back of
Tom's head, stunning him as he fell
among the mud and grass. One more
hit like that, and Tom would have no
fight left in him.

Feeling as if he were in some kind
of horrible cat-and-mouse game, he
struggled once more to his feet and
ran after the Beast, his sword raised.

His hand hurt more than ever. Hawkite was clever; she flew so close to him that he could almost touch her with the tip of his sword – but not quite. There was no way he would be able to climb onto her back. As long as the Beast had him in her sights, she wasn't going to let him near her.

In her sights... The ring! Tom forced himself to stop running. He closed his eyes and made himself as still as he could. *Please work!* he willed. He knew his life depended on it. Hawkite's merciless talons would tear him open, given half the chance.

He stood, frozen to the spot, and waited for the Beast to come to him.

CHAPTER EIGHT

DISAPPEARING ACT

Hawkite pulled her wings into her sides and dived towards Tom. Staying still was almost impossible. As he watched, Tom could feel himself being drawn into those terrible red eyes. He imagined the razor-sharp talons reaching out and ripping him apart... Blinking hard, he forced himself to remain where he was,

focussing on the great talons falling
towards him.

Hawkite stopped in confusion.
Pulling out of her dive, she wheeled
away. Her glowing eyes raked the
field like fire. Throwing back her
vile head, she screamed. She'd lost
her prey.

Tom felt exultant. The magic had worked! He wanted to cheer, but it would give away his position. Out of the corner of his eye, he spotted Elenna punching the air in triumph at his disappearing act. Holding his breath, he began moving very slowly as the Beast screamed and swooped lower. He needed to confuse her again. How fast could he move before Hawkite saw him this time?

The Beast was coming in to land. Tom braced his feet, feeling determined. He steadied himself against the gust of reeking wind as the bird glided down to land a few arm-spans away. Once again, he caught a glimpse of the strange green feathers as Hawkite folded her wings and settled on the dirt. *That's it!* Tom realised that Velmal was using those feathers to control the

giant bird. He must remove them. The
Beast snapped her head round, left
and right. Her glowing eyes looked
like they were seeking out her
invisible prey.

Closer and closer she came. Tom was
within a sword's length of her now.

This is my only chance, he thought. He
remembered the starving faces of the
villagers and knew he had to free
Hawkite from the evil magic of Velmal.
Holding his sword as tightly as he
could, he brought it down towards the
Beast's wing. The air whistled. Tom saw
his arm materialise in the sudden fast
movement. He was visible again.

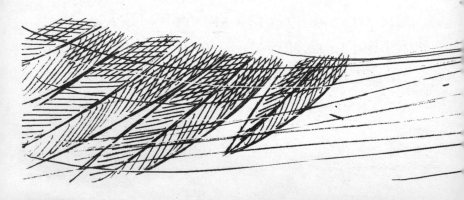

The Beast turned like lightning.
She fixed her blazing eyes on Tom
with a look of hatred on her face.
He reared back as she darted her
ugly head forward. The Beast
shrieked, and beat her wings
powerfully. Tom was sent flying
back by the power of the wind.

He scrambled to his feet as quickly as he could. Now that the Beast could see him again, it was only a matter of time before she would slice him in half with her ferocious beak.

The only way Tom could use this new magic was to continue confusing Hawkite and tire her out. Appear – disappear – appear again. Where she least expected him. He only needed to keep it up long enough to reach those glowing green feathers and tear them out. He had seen enough evil magic now to know that those feathers held the key.

Tom raced away from the Beast. He stumbled in the powerful wind as Hawkite rose into the air. She chased him down the avenues of broken cornstalks. He veered and darted – then froze. Glancing down at himself,

he couldn't help grinning. He'd
disappeared again.

Hawkite pulled abruptly out of her
dive. She rose into the sky and
wheeled about, searching.

"While there's blood in my veins,
I will free you from this curse," Tom
muttered to himself. And once again
he set off quickly across the field, in
the opposite direction.

Hawkite came after him like an
arrow. Tom raced on. He dodged and
ducked. Stinking black feathers
brushed across the shield he wore
across his back. The razor-like beak
snapped – and missed. Tom had
dropped to the ground to lie as still as
a stone, disappearing once more.

Hawkite rose into the air with a
terrible croak of defeated rage. Tom
moved his head slowly. He saw

Elenna on the edge of the field with her arrows at the ready, Storm and Silver by her side. If Tom could lure Hawkite closer, Elenna might have half a chance of helping him defeat the Beast!

Silver was barking madly. Storm paced the verge, tossing his head. Taking a chance, Hawkite swooped – even though she clearly had no idea where Tom was. She lashed out blindly with one of her gleaming talons. It whistled past Tom like a scythe, missing him by a whisker. Tom swallowed and tried not to think about how close he had just come to losing a limb.

Once the Beast was safely past, Tom broke into a run again. Exhausted, he zigzagged towards the edge of the field, where he could see Elenna

looking down the shaft of her arrow,
following the Beast's movements.
Hawkite shrieked with frustration,
banking away as Elenna released an
arrow straight at the Beast's wing.

And then Tom stumbled, jerking
forwards. As he sprawled in the mud,
he knew one thing with deadly
certainty.

He was at Hawkite's mercy.

CHAPTER NINE

CURSED FEATHERS

Tom felt the rush of wind as Hawkite closed in. He could hear Elenna's arrows whistling over his head. Silver's barking was lost in the tornado-like gusts that threatened to pick him up and slam him back down to the ground. Tom waited for Hawkite's attack. Would he end up like the hapless farmer who lay dead and broken at the far side of the field? Then the Beast's beak would dart in, ripping at his skin...

With one final effort, Tom raised his head. The Beast was bringing in her wings as her talons reached out for him. The cursed green feathers blazed. They were almost within reach. If he could just jump before she folded them away completely...

Tom reached deep within himself. He thought of his father Taladon, and all that Avantia's Master of the Beasts had been through to keep Avantia safe. He thought of King Hugo, who had placed so much faith in him on these Quests. He thought of the starving people of Gwildor, and his faithful friends calling his name and urging him on.

Bunching up his legs, Tom leapt.

"That's it, Tom!" he heard Elenna call, her voice jubilant. His arms reached up high – and his fingers closed on the green feathers. They were hot, burning his fingers like acid. The Beast screamed in pain as Tom pulled. She pushed up and away from the ground, snapping fiercely at Tom with her beak. But she couldn't bring her head around far enough to reach him. Tom hung on. The ground fell away far below as he was lifted into the air, clutching onto Hawkite's massive wing.

But the feathers wouldn't budge. Tom could feel the evil magic blistering his fingers as he tugged. The pain in his sword-hand from Krabb's bite was overwhelming. If the feathers came out now, he would fall, perhaps to his death. But he had to do it. The fate of Gwildor – and Avantia too – depended on him!

Now Elenna, Silver and Storm were tiny dots on the ground. The thatched roofs of the village beyond were like little golden sequins gleaming in the sun. Tom thought he might faint from the pain and the stench of the Beast as Hawkite snapped her beak at him again and again. She flew in circles, tighter and tighter. Tom was getting dizzy and his shoulders screamed with pain as he clutched onto Hawkite. He gave one last savage tug.

"While there's blood in my veins…" he muttered. The feathers came away from Hawkite's body and then Tom was falling, spiralling down through the air.

With a massive effort, Tom reached around for his shield and the magic eagle's feather that lay embedded in its battle-scarred surface. He felt his descent begin to slow. The magic was working.

Far above, Hawkite was whirling in joyful circles, calling out. She sounded different. She sounded free.

Tom landed gently on the ground, his knees crumpling beneath him.

"Tom!" Elenna ran towards him, half-laughing and half-crying. In the background, Silver was chasing his tail like a cub. "We thought you were never coming down. Oh, Tom, you did it!"

Tom grinned. "*We* did it," he corrected.

He rubbed the dirt from the magic tokens that had come to his aid so many times. Then he slung the shield back over his shoulder. Storm nuzzled his warm velvety nose into Tom's neck. It tickled. Tom laughed, and lifted his arm to stroke his stallion's mane. His other hand still clutched at the feathers he had pulled from Hawkite's wing. They looked so innocent. Tom could tell, as the feathers lay cool and smooth in his fingers, that the evil magic had gone forever.

There was a strange stirring in the soil beneath Tom. He stood up, sinking his fingers into Silver's warm fur to steady himself. He and Elenna watched with surprise as the broken crops around them began to pull themselves upright. A healthy golden glow flowed up the cornstalks as they straightened. Fresh ears of corn bloomed before their eyes.

"It's magic," Elenna murmured, fingering the new corn as it fattened and ripened around them. The whole

field was back to the way it had been before the enchanted Beast had destroyed it.

Far overhead, Hawkite wheeled lazily. Her harsh cries had given way to joyous song. She was back, patrolling the skies where she belonged and protecting the land she loved.

Velmal's curse was broken once again.

CHAPTER TEN

TOM'S TRUE DESTINY

At the foot of the tree on the far side
of the field, Tom and Elenna both
saw the prone body of the farmer stir
and get groggily to his feet. A young
boy ran towards him from behind
some fencing. Their cries of delight
drifted on the breeze towards Tom
and Elenna as the boy was swung up
into his father's arms.

Villagers had appeared at the side of the field. They gazed in disbelief as their crops returned to their former glory. Fallen trees leaped upright. Fruit fattened on branches, even as the branches straightened and healed themselves. One boy hesitantly reached for a cluster of glossy fresh blackberries that had burst from the hedgerow. He tasted them carefully, as if he were afraid they would vanish in his hand.

"How...?"

"The land is healed!"

"Food!"

Elenna laughed as the boy with the blackberries ran up to her and put his arms around her waist. Everywhere, there were smiling faces and whoops of delight.

"Thank you," came a voice at the

back of the cheering crowd. "How can we ever repay you?"

Tom and Elenna watched as the big villager who had threatened Tom with a knife pushed through to the front. He knelt hesitantly before Tom.

"I don't know how you have done this," he said, "but I know you have restored Gwildor. You have brought us fresh hope. And I held a knife to your throat! I don't know what to say."

Tom pulled him back to his feet. "Say nothing," he said. "Truly. It's forgotten."

"A feast!" shouted the old woman who had shown them the strange painting. "You will be our guests. But we must prepare!"

A burst of chatter broke out among the crowd as the villagers turned away and hurried out of the field.

Snatches of conversation drifted back towards Tom and Elenna.

"Apples! Pears! Berries! All the colours of the Gwildor harvest...!"

Tom and Elenna watched them go. A small thud on the ground by Tom's feet made him look down. The magic pearl he had given to the villagers to save them from starvation had been returned to him. He bent down and picked it up, wincing at the pain in his sword hand. The bruise had spread further. Determined not to worry, Tom studied the pearl instead. It was as heavy and beautiful as ever, and felt good to have in his hand once more. He would never let it out of his sight again.

"Thank goodness for Freya's ring," Elenna murmured. She took hold of

Tom's hand and examined the golden band on his little finger.

As Tom thought about Gwildor's enchanted Mistress of the Beasts, darkness fell around him.
The air grew icy. An invisible force picked him up and slammed him to the ground. Silver yelped, and he felt Storm buck and rear beside him. Tom barely had time to draw breath before Freya appeared.

Her long hair whipped around her head and shoulders, like thick black snakes. Standing in her armour, she was a fearsome sight, her face twisted with fury. And yet... Tom wanted to help her.

"While there's blood in my veins, I'll free you, Freya," Tom said, holding the Mistress of the Beasts' fiery gaze.

"I don't *want* to be free!" Freya
hissed. Her eyes burned into him with
hate. But Tom didn't look away. "Don't
you understand? Gwildor is nothing to
me. Velmal is my Master now!"

Tom felt a pain in his heart. He
reached out his hand to the woman in
front of him. Freya stepped back,
sneering. "You won't succeed in this
Quest," she snarled. "Krabb and
Hawkite were nothing. Are you ready
for Rokk, the Walking Mountain? No,
Tom. No one can conquer *him*. Leave

Gwildor now, while you still can!"

The air swirled and eddied. Then the darkness lifted. Once again, Tom, Elenna, Storm and Silver were alone in the dazzling Gwildor light. Tom turned to look at Elenna. She stood with her fingers twisting uncertainly through Silver's thick fur.

"Is this Quest too much, Tom?" she asked in a worried voice. "Have we started something we can't finish?"

Tom shook his head forcefully. "Never," he said through gritted teeth. "Whatever Freya might say, I'm not turning back. I can't explain it, Elenna, but this Quest feels like my true destiny." He lifted his sword high in the air. "And I'll *never* turn away from that!"

Here's a sneak preview of Tom's
next exciting adventure!

Meet

ROKK
THE WALKING
MOUNTAIN

Only Tom can free the Beasts from
Velmal's wicked enchantment...

PROLOGUE

"Home!" Briel gasped, as he reached the peak of the North Mountain. The village of Tion spilled out across the valley below him.

He paused to catch his breath and give his aching legs time to recover. Stone huts with thatched roofs lined the dusty brown roads linking the North and South Mountains that loomed over Tion.

It was Market Day. Briel knew that traders from all over Northern Gwildor would be making their way to Tion.

Behind him, he heard a chorus of bleating. He glanced over his shoulder at the herd of goats he'd driven from the nearby town of Kewas. It was Briel's job to make sure that none of the animals were lost during the trip across the treacherous mountains.

He looked back at Tion. Memories of his sister's cooking made his stomach rumble. After a week of eating nothing more than honey-cakes, a freshly roasted chicken was just what he needed.

"Why am I wasting time?" he wondered.

"Let's get home!"

As Briel strode forwards, he heard a low, grating sound – like rock scraping across rock. He felt vibrations beneath his feet and paused, head cocked, listening carefully.

Faint voices suddenly sounded from below: "Flee! Get away!"

Briel scrambled back to the top of the peak for a better view. Down in Tion, it was chaos – tiny figures of bolting horses threw riders; mothers and fathers scooped up young children; traders bundled up as many of their wares as they could carry. Everyone was running.

Briel narrowed his eyes, trying to pick out his sister among the crowds. Where was she? Please let her be safe, he thought.

A blur of movement on the far mountain suddenly caught his attention.

"Avalanche!" Briel gasped.

Dozens of boulders tumbled down the South Mountain, smashing into the ground and careering in every direction, gaining speed. They crashed into homes, sending bricks and wooden beams flying. It was the most ferocious avalanche Briel had ever seen. Then, suddenly, the momentum of the rocks came to a halt, freezing them to the spot.

Follow this Quest to the end in ROKK THE WALKING MOUNTAIN.

Win an exclusive
Beast Quest T-shirt and goody bag!

Tom has battled many fearsome Beasts and we want to know which one is your favourite! Send us a drawing or painting of your favourite Beast and tell us in 30 words why you think it's the best.

Each month we will select **three** winners to receive a Beast Quest T-shirt and goody bag!

Send your entry on a postcard to
BEAST QUEST COMPETITION
Orchard Books, 338 Euston Road, London NW1 3BH.

Australian readers should email:
childrens.books@hachette.com.au

New Zealand readers should write to:
Beast Quest Competition, PO Box 3255, Shortland St, Auckland 1140, NZ or email: childrensbooks@hachette.co.nz

**Don't forget to include your name and address.
Only one entry per child.**

Good luck!

Fight the Beasts,
Fear the Magic

www.beastquest.co.uk

Have you checked out the Beast Quest website?
It's the place to go for games, downloads, activities,
sneak previews and lots of fun!

You can read all about your favourite beasts,
download free screensavers and desktop wallpapers
for your computer, and even challenge your friends
to a Beast Tournament.

Sign up to the newsletter at www.beastquest.co.uk
to receive exclusive extra content and the
opportunity to enter special members-only
competitions. We'll send you up-to-date info on all
the Beast Quest books, including the next exciting
series which features four brand-new Beasts!

FREE COLLECTOR CARDS INSIDE!

Series 5
BEAST QUEST

Tom must travel to Gwildor, Avantia's twin kingdom, to free six new Beasts from an evil enchantment...

978 1 40830 437 2

978 1 40830 438 9

978 1 40830 439 6

978 1 40830 440 2

978 1 40830 441 9

978 1 40830 442 6

978 1 40830 436 5

SPECIAL BUMPER EDITION!

Can Tom rescue the precious Cup of Life from a deadly two-headed demon?

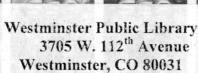